Best-loved Stories & Nursery Rhymes

For Lily

Ian Beck

Best-loved Stories & Nursery Rhymes

OXFORD

UNIVERSITY PRESS

Contents

Lazy Jack

Once upon a time, a long time ago, when the world was still full of marvels, there was a boy called Jack. He lived with his mother at the edge of a fine country town. They were very poor, and Jack's mother did as best she could, and worked very hard for their living. She knitted woollen socks for all the local gentry. She worked from dawn till dusk, wearing out her poor old fingers. Her son Jack, on the other hand, did nothing. During the hot summer months he would sit around in the garden, fanning himself.

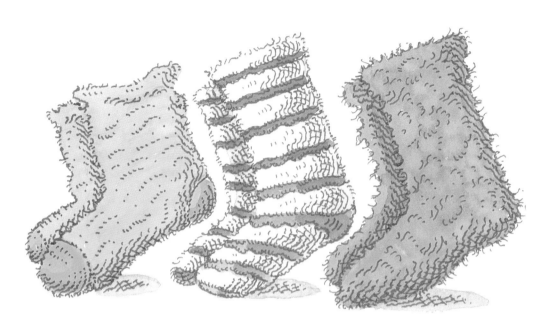

Then he would hog the best of the fireplace during the long cold winters.

Everyone shook their heads and called him Lazy Jack. His mother did her best, but she could never persuade him to lift a finger to help. Finally, one day she said that, 'enough was enough'. He must go out and work to help pay his way, or she would turn him into the street, and no one would want to help Lazy Jack!

Now this worried Jack, and bright and early the next morning he set off for a nearby farm. There he was hired to help, and at the end of the day he was paid with a shiny new penny. Jack walked home slowly in the evening sun. He spun his penny up in the air and generally showed it off to everyone, for he had never earned a whole penny before.

When he was nearly home, Jack lost the penny. It dropped in the water as he crossed the stream. His mother shook her head. 'I knew you were lazy, Jack, now it turns out you're daft as well. You should have put that penny safely in your pocket.'

'I will remember next time,' sighed Jack.

So early the next morning Jack set out and was given a job helping with the cows. At the end of the day, Jack was paid with a handsome jug of creamy fresh milk. Jack remembered what had happened to his penny. So he put the jug of milk deep into his trouser pocket, and set off home. By the time he got there, he had spilled all the milk, and the jug was empty.

'Oh dear me, Jack,' said his mother, 'what will become of you? You should have carried that on your silly head.'

'I will remember next time,' said Jack.

The next morning Jack set off in good heart to another farm. He was given a day's work helping in the dairy. At the end of the day, Jack was paid with a great round of delicious cream cheese.

'Mother will be pleased,' thought Jack, and, remembering what had happened to the milk in his pocket, he popped the round of soft cheese on top of his head and set off in the warm evening sun to walk home.

By the time he got home the cheese had melted and spoiled. It had run into his hair, and all down his shirt in a great sticky mess.

'I don't know, Jack,' said his mother. 'What a waste. Your shirt's ruined, and as for your hair, I can't even look. You should have carried that fine cheese carefully in your hands.'

'Sorry, mother,' said Jack. 'I will remember next time.'

The next morning Jack set out at cock-crow and was given a day's work by the baker. Jack worked hard all day in the hot bakery, and the baker paid him with a fine ginger tom-cat. Now Jack remembered what had happened to the cream cheese, so he took the tom-cat and began to carry it home very carefully in his hands. But this was a fierce and proud cat, and it began to yowl, and wriggle, and scratch. So much so that Jack had to let it go.

When he got home his mother could scarcely believe it. 'My word Jack, but you are a nincompoop. You should have tied a string around the cat and pulled 'im along behind you.'

'Sorry, mother,' said Jack. 'I will remember next time.'

Early the following morning, Jack found work from the butcher, and at the end of the day the butcher paid Jack with a fine ham on the bone. Now his mother would be pleased, it was just the thing to serve with a boiled cabbage. Then Jack remembered what had happened to the cat, so he tied a piece of string to the ham and pulled it all the way home behind him, through all the mud, and mess, and muddle of the streets. By the time he got home, of course, there was barely a shank of bone left at the end of the string: the ham was ruined.

His mother finally lost her temper, and fetched him a clout on the head. 'You're as daft as a brush. Now we've just cabbage for our dinner. You should have carried it on your shoulder.'

'Ow,' said Jack. 'Sorry, mother. I will remember next time.'

The next day Jack was hired by a wealthy merchant, who lived in a fine house nearby. Now this merchant was a widower who had a beautiful daughter. The daughter was very sad; she had neither laughed nor spoken for many years. All that week she had seen Jack from her window as he went off to his various jobs. Every evening she had watched him come home again.

She had seen him lose his penny in the stream. She had seen him with milk spilling from his pocket. She had seen him with a great cream cheese melting into his hair. She had seen him struggling with a fierce tom-cat.

She had seen him pulling a ham through the streets on a piece of string. Each time she had felt a little cheered up by the sight of Lazy Jack. (He was, after all, not a bad looking lad.) She could feel herself thawing inside like the river at the end of a long winter.

At the end of the day, the merchant rewarded Jack with a fine young donkey. Now Jack remembered what had happened to the ham, and with a great effort he swung the donkey up on to his shoulders. He began to stagger home with it. The merchant's daughter saw Jack from her window. He looked so silly trudging along with the donkey upside down across his shoulders and with its legs sticking up above his head, that she burst into great peals of golden laughter.

The merchant was so delighted to have his daughter restored to her old self that he sent for Jack and rewarded him with a gold sovereign. Jack straightaway put the sovereign in his pocket to keep it safe. Later in the year Jack married the merchant's beautiful daughter, and his mother was able to retire from knitting socks. She lived with them in their fine house, for the rest of her days, which was a very long time indeed.

Boys and Girls Come Out to Play

Boys and girls come out to play,
The moon doth shine as bright as day,
Leave your supper and leave your sleep,
And join your playfellows in the street.
Come with a whoop and come with a call,
Come with a good will or not at all.
Up the ladder and down the wall,
A half-penny loaf will serve us all;
You find milk and I'll find flour,
And we'll have a pudding in half an hour.

Sally Go Round the Sun

Sally go round the sun,
Sally go round the moon,
Sally go round the chimney-pots
On a Saturday afternoon.

Clap Hands

Clap hands, Daddy comes
With his pocket full of plums,
And a cake for Johnny.

The Swing

How do you like to go up in a swing,
Up in the air so blue?
Oh, I do think it the pleasantest thing
Ever a child can do!

Up in the air and over the wall,
Till I can see so wide.
Rivers and trees and cattle and all
Over the countryside—

Till I look down on the garden green,
Down on the roof so brown—
Up in the air I go flying again,
Up in the air and down!

Robert Louis Stevenson

Bed in Summer

In winter I get up at night
And dress by yellow candle-light.
In summer, quite the other way,
I have to go to bed by day.

I have to go to bed and see
The birds still hopping on the tree,
Or hear the grown-up people's feet
Still going past me in the street.

And does it not seem hard to you
When all the sky is clear and blue,
And I should like so much to play,
To have to got to bed by day?

Robert Louis Stevenson

The Tortoise and
the Hare

Once upon a time, and as long ago as anyone can remember, there lived a tortoise. His was a slow, steady, and pleasant life. Every winter, while the world was cold and harsh, he would fill up on sweet lettuce and carrots, and then fall fast asleep in his cosy home, until the spring.

Just near the tortoise lived an excitable and bouncy hare. He rushed everywhere at great speed, especially in the spring, when he seemed to be full of extra energy.

So it was one spring morning, when the hare rushed past his neighbour the tortoise on the road. The tortoise had been ambling along, minding his own business. He had only just woken up from his long winter sleep, and was just getting used to the world again, when he was nearly knocked over by the dashing hare.

'Hey, watch where you are going,' said the tortoise. 'We can't all rush about like you.'

'My word,' said the hare, 'but you are a slowcoach.'

Now the tortoise was cross at having been nearly knocked over, and he answered quite snappily, 'Not as slow as you seem to think. Why, I could beat you in a race any day.'

'Oh, really,' said the hare with a laugh. 'I wouldn't bet on it if I were you.'

Just then a fox strolled past, and the hare said, 'This tortoise says he can beat me in a race,' and they both laughed, so that the tortoise got even crosser.

He said, 'I bet you my snug winter den that I can beat you over any distance.'

'I'll bet you a lifetime supply of sweet lettuce and carrots that you can't,' said the hare.

Then the fox said, 'You shall run a race, and I shall judge the winner.'

'Agreed,' said the tortoise and the hare together, and the hare added, 'Easiest bet I've ever won,' and laughed again. The tortoise said nothing, just smiled and shook his head.

So it was that the fox set up a course across the countryside with a start and finish line, and on a bright morning the tortoise and the hare lined up ready to start.

The fox raised his flag, and said, 'Ready,' and the hare raised himself up on his strong back legs, while the tortoise just stood and waited. Then the fox said, 'Steady,' and the hare breathed heavily and puffed out his cheeks, running on the spot, while the tortoise just stood and waited. Then the fox said 'Go!' and dropped the flag, and the hare sprinted away as fast as he could, while the tortoise just ambled forward in a slow and steady way.

The hare ran fast for a while. Then he slowed a little and looked back down the road. There was no sign of the tortoise, he had been left far behind. The hare laughed to himself and stopped altogether. It was a warm morning, and running so fast was tiring work. The hare spotted a nice patch of shade under a tree, and he went and sat there to wait for the tortoise.

'It'll be a long wait,' he said, and yawned and stretched. 'I'll just have a little nap.' So the hare settled under the tree and soon fell fast asleep.

The tortoise meanwhile was walking along, not fast, but sure and steady. As it was so warm, and he was hot inside his shell, he stopped and had a nibble of some cooling dandelion leaves, and a drink from a stream. The sun rose higher and hotter, and he ambled on, slow but sure. After what seemed a very long time he drew level with, and then just overtook, a snail. 'Morning, Mr Snail,' said the tortoise.

'Morning, Mr Tortoise,' said the snail. 'If you look over there you can see the hare asleep under that tree.'

'Why, so he is,' said the tortoise, and he shook his head and carried on, and on, down the dusty road.

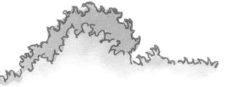

The hare woke from his refreshing nap. He felt fine, if a little stiff. He stretched and ran up and down for a bit, to ease himself in for the run. Then he climbed the tree and looked back down the road. There was no sign of the tortoise but he could just see a snail, far away on the road. He turned round and he could see the road going the other way, and far off he could see the finish line with the bright banner, and a crowd of animals waiting. He was about to jump down and do some push-ups before setting off again, when he saw something on the road that caused him to fall down from the tree in shock. It was the tortoise plodding along, only yards from the finish line.

The hare picked himself up, and set off again as fast as he could. He crested the hill at great speed, and there, some way ahead of him, was the tortoise, making steady progress, and now only a few feet from the finish line. The hare made a great effort and charged down the final straight. He crossed the line and fell out of breath to the ground. He was too late. The tortoise had crossed the line long before the hare, and was being congratulated by the fox.

'That's a lifetime of sweet lettuce and carrots that the hare owes me,' said the tortoise, with a big smile. 'You see, hare, slow and steady does it.'

And the tortoise lived for a very, very, very long time (as tortoises do) and for all of that time the hare had to make sure he had lots and lots of sweet lettuce and carrots. Except during the long cold winter, of course, when the tortoise was snug and asleep in his burrow, and the hare had all that long, cold time to himself.

The Brave Old Duke of York

Oh, the brave old Duke of York,
He had ten thousand men;
He marched them up to the top of the hill,
And then he marched them down again.
And when they were up, they were up,
And when they were down, they were down,
And when they were only halfway up,
They were neither up nor down.

Sing a Song of Sixpence

Sing a song of sixpence,
    A pocket full of rye;
Four and twenty blackbirds,
    Baked in a pie.

When the pie was opened,
    The birds began to sing;
Was not that a dainty dish,
    To set before the king?

The king was in his counting-house,
Counting out his money;
The queen was in the parlour,
Eating bread and honey.

The maid was in the garden,
Hanging out the clothes,
When down came a blackbird
And pecked off her nose.

Hickory, Dickory, Dock

Hickory, dickory, dock,
The mouse ran up the clock.
The clock struck one,
The mouse ran down,
Hickory, dickory, dock.

Polly Put the Kettle On

Polly put the kettle on,
Polly put the kettle on,
Polly put the kettle on,
We'll all have tea.

Sukey take it off again,
Sukey take it off again,
Sukey take it off again,
They've all gone away.

Round and Round the Garden

Round and round the garden
Like a teddy bear;
One step, two step,
Tickle you under there!

Ride a Cock-Horse

Ride a cock-horse to Banbury Cross,
To see a fine lady upon a white horse;
Rings on her fingers and bells on her toes,
And she shall have music wherever she goes.

Teasing

Little Jack Horner sat in the corner
Eating his curds and whey.
There came a big spider,
Who sat down beside him,
And the dish ran away with the spoon.
Ha-Ha.

Incey Wincey Spider

Incey Wincey spider
Climbing up the spout;

Down came the rain
And washed the spider out;

Out came the sun
And dried up all the rain;

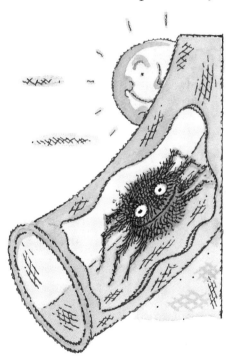

Incey Wincey spider
Climbing up again.

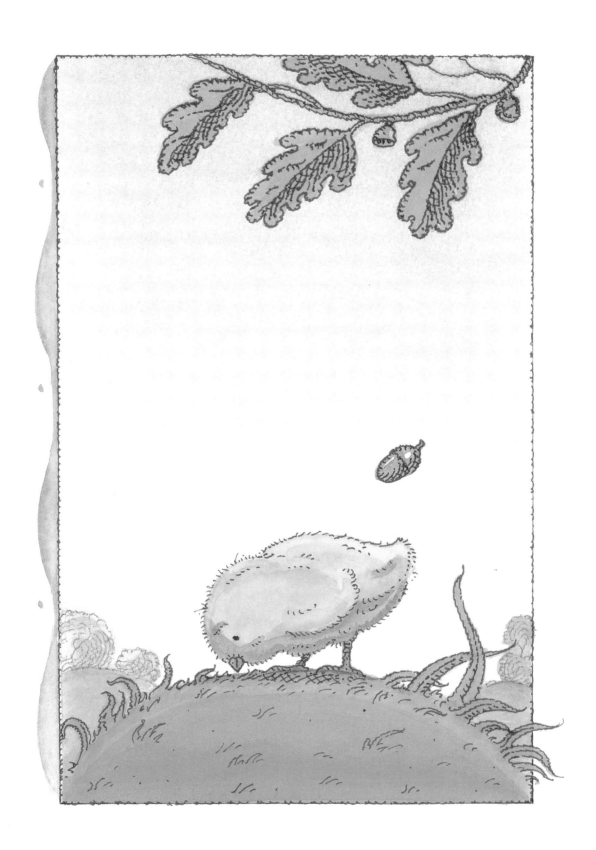

Chicken Licken

Once upon a time, when the world was young and the animals could speak, there was a tiny wee chick called Chicken Licken. Now it happened that fluffy, yellow Chicken Licken was grubbing about in her favourite patch, when an acorn fell, 'plomp', on her little tail. 'Oh no,' said Chicken Licken, 'the sky is falling down. Help, I must go and warn the king.'

So she set off on her busy little feet, and after a while she met her great friend Henny Penny.

'Well well, if it isn't Chicken Licken,' said Henny Penny. 'Where are you off to in such a hurry?'

'Quick, help help, Henny Penny. The sky is falling down, and I must go and warn the king.'

'I see,' said Henny Penny. 'And how can you be so sure that the sky is falling down?'

'Because,' said Chicken Licken, 'I saw it with my own two eyes, heard it with my own two ears, and a piece of the sky landed, plomp, on my own tail.'

'Then I'll come with you,' said Henny Penny.

So they set off together, and tripped along through the grass, until they met Cocky Locky.

'Well, a-doodle well,' said Cocky Locky to Henny Penny and Chicken Licken. 'Where are you two going, may I ask a-doodle do?'

'Oh, help, Cocky Locky. The sky is falling down, and we must go and warn the king.'

'I see,' said Cocky Locky. 'And how do you know the sky is falling a-doodle down?'

'Chicken Licken told me,' said Henny Penny.

'I saw it with my own two eyes, heard it with my own two ears, and a piece of the sky landed, plomp, on my tail,' said Chicken Licken.

'Very well,' said Cocky Locky, 'I will travel with you, and we will warn the king.'

So all three set off skipping through the grass, until they met Ducky Daddles.

'Well, well, well, quack, well,' said Ducky Daddles. 'If it isn't Cocky Locky, Henny Penny, and Chicken Licken. Where are you all off to?'

'Oh, help a-doodle do, the sky is falling down, and we must go and warn the king.'

'But how do you know the sky is falling down?' asked Ducky Daddles.

'Well, Henny Penny told me,' said Cocky Locky.

'Yes, and Chicken Licken told me,' said Henny Penny.

'I saw it with my own two eyes, heard it with my own two ears, and a piece of it landed, plomp, on my own tail,' said Chicken Licken.

'Then I had better, quack, come with you, and we can all warn the king.'

So they set off together, on their brisk little feet, until they met Goosey Loosey.

'A very good morning to you, Ducky Daddles, Cocky Locky, Henny Penny, and Chicken Licken. Where might you all be going in such a rush?'

'Oh, help, Goosey Loosey, the sky is falling down and we must go and warn the king.'

'But how do you know that the sky is falling down?' asked Goosey Loosey, looking up at the bright blue above.

'Cocky Locky told me,' said Ducky Daddles.

'Henny Penny told me,' said Cocky Locky.

'Chicken Licken told me,' said Henny Penny.

'I saw it with my own two eyes, I heard it with my own two ears, and a piece of it landed, plomp, on my own tail,' said Chicken Licken.

'I think I had better come with you, and together we can all warn the king,' said Goosey Loosey.

So they all set off in a busy little line, until they met Turkey Lurkey.

'Goodness gracious me,' said Turkey Lurkey. 'Goosey Loosey, Ducky Daddles, Cocky Locky, Henny Penny, and Chicken Licken! What a fine feathered sight on such a morning. Where are you all trotting off to?'

'Oh, you must help us, Turkey Lurkey. The sky is falling down, and we must go and warn the king.'

'But how do you know the sky is falling down?' said Turkey Lurkey.

'Ducky Daddles told me,' said Goosey Loosey.

'Cocky Locky told me,' said Ducky Daddles.

'Henny Penny told me,' said Cocky Locky.

'Chicken Licken told me,' said Henny Penny.

'I saw it with my own two eyes, and heard it with my own two ears, and a piece of it landed, plomp, on my own tail,' said Chicken Licken.

'I think I had better come with you. Yes, that's the best thing, then we can all warn the king together,' said Turkey Lurkey.

So off they all went, smallest in front, biggest at the back, until they met Mr Foxy Woxy.

'Mmmm, good morning,' said Mr Foxy Woxy. 'Well, well, if it isn't Turkey Lurkey, Goosey Loosey, Ducky Daddles, Cocky Locky, Henny Penny, and Chicken Licken. Where are you all going to on such a fine morning?'

'Oh, help, Mr Foxy Woxy. The sky is falling down, and we must go and warn the king!'

'But how do you know the sky is falling down?' asked Mr Foxy Woxy.

'Goosey Loosey told me,' said Turkey Lurkey.

'Ducky Daddles told me,' said Goosey Loosey.

'Cocky Locky told me,' said Ducky Daddles.

'Henny Penny told me,' said Cocky Locky.

'Chicken Licken told me,' said Henny Penny.

'I saw it with my own two eyes, and heard it with my own two ears, and a piece of it landed, plomp, on my own tail,' said Chicken Licken.

'Then we shall all run together as fast as we can to my little den, for safety, and then I will warn the king,' said Mr Foxy Woxy.

So all together they scurried on their busy little feet into the dark den of Mr Foxy Woxy. And so it was that the king was never warned that the sky was falling down.

I Saw a Ship A-Sailing

I saw a ship a-sailing,
A-sailing on the sea;
And oh! it was laden
With pretty things for me.

There were comfits in the cabin,
And apples in the hold;
The sails were made of silk,
And the masts were made of gold.

The four-and-twenty sailors
That stood between the decks,
Were four-and-twenty white mice,
With chains about their necks.

The Captain was a duck,
With a packet on his back,
And when the ship began to move,
The Captain said, 'Quack, quack!'

Bobby Shaftoe

Bobby Shaftoe's gone to sea,
Silver buckles at his knee;
He'll come back and marry me,
    Bonny Bobby Shaftoe.

Row, Row, Row Your Boat

Row, row, row your boat,
Gently down the stream,
Merrily, merrily, merrily, merrily,
Life is but a dream.

Three Wise Men

Three wise men of Gotham
Went to sea in a bowl;
If the bowl had been stronger,
My story would have been longer.

Rub-a-Dub-Dub

Rub-a-dub-dub,
Three men in a tub,
And who do you think they were?
The butcher, the baker,
The candlestick-maker,
All going to the fair.

The Herring

The herring loves the merry moonlight
And the mackerel loves the wind,
But the oyster loves the dredging song
For he comes of a gentle kind.

Dance to Your Daddy

Dance to your daddy,
  My little babby,
Dance to your daddy,
  My little lamb.
You shall have a fishy
  In a little dishy,
You shall have a fishy
  When the boat comes in.
You shall have an apple,
  You shall have a plum,
You shall have a rattle-basket
  When your daddy comes home.

Where Go the Boats?

Dark brown is the river,
Golden is the sand.
It flows along for ever,
With trees on either hand.

Green leaves a-floating,
Castles of the foam,
Boats of mine a-boating—
Where will all come home?

On goes the river
And out past the mill,
Away down the valley,
Away down the hill.

Away down the river,
A hundred miles or more,
Other little children
Shall bring my boats ashore.

Robert Louis Stevenson

The Porridge Pot

Once upon a time, when the world was a place of forests and magic, there lived a little girl called Ragamuffin. She lived with her mother, in a tiny wooden house, in a tiny village on the edge of a great dark forest. Her mother was very poor, and did the best she could to feed and clothe herself and her little daughter.

However, as autumn ended, and the cold and darkness of winter approached, things went from bad to worse. At last the larder was bare, and there was nothing left for them to eat.

'Don't worry, mother,' said kind little Ragamuffin. 'There may be a few berries left in among the trees. I'll see if I can find some.' And so Ragamuffin set out with her basket on her arm. She walked among the tall trees. It was damp and misty, and gradually Ragamuffin found herself walking deeper and deeper along the twisty paths. She found no berries, no mushrooms, no nuts, nothing.

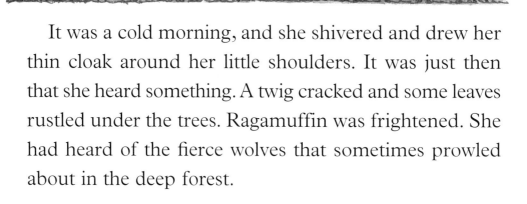

It was a cold morning, and she shivered and drew her thin cloak around her little shoulders. It was just then that she heard something. A twig cracked and some leaves rustled under the trees. Ragamuffin was frightened. She had heard of the fierce wolves that sometimes prowled about in the deep forest.

But then she heard a friendly voice. 'Is that you, my little Ragamuffin?' And an old lady appeared, leaning on a stout walking stick. She stepped forward from the mist under the trees. 'I know you, little Ragamuffin,' she said.

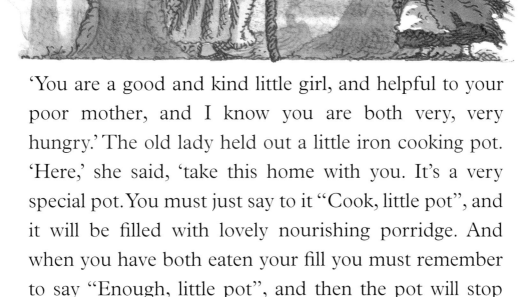

'You are a good and kind little girl, and helpful to your poor mother, and I know you are both very, very hungry.' The old lady held out a little iron cooking pot. 'Here,' she said, 'take this home with you. It's a very special pot. You must just say to it "Cook, little pot", and it will be filled with lovely nourishing porridge. And when you have both eaten your fill you must remember to say "Enough, little pot", and then the pot will stop making the porridge.'

Ragamuffin took the pot and thanked the old lady. Then she ran back home to her mother as fast as she could, clutching the little pot under her cloak.

When she arrived back at the little house, her mother was sitting at the table, her head sunk in despair. Ragamuffin set the little pot on the bare wooden table. 'Cook, little pot,' she said. At once the kitchen filled with the smell of fresh, warm porridge. Her mother looked up. There was a friendly bubbly sound, and the little pot filled to the brim with what looked like steaming porridge. It was the most delicious porridge they had ever tasted, just sweet enough, and tasting as though it were made with cream fresh from the cow. They ate and ate until they could eat no more. Ragamuffin said, 'Enough, little pot,' and the pot was empty again.

For most of that long, cold winter, Ragamuffin and her mother ate together from the little pot. The porridge stayed as fresh and delicious as ever. Then, one day, Ragamuffin's mother was alone in the house. She thought it could do no harm to have some of the delicious porridge on her own. She fetched the little pot down from its special shelf, and set it down on the table.

She waited for a moment in anticipation, and then said, 'Cook, little pot.' There came the familiar delicious smell, then the little bubbly noise, and then the pot was full, and the mother ate her fill, and then a little more, and then even some more, so that her tummy was nicely warm and rounded. Then the mother closed her eyes in contentment, and fell fast asleep.

She woke up a little later, with the feeling that her chair was afloat on a warm sea. She opened her eyes, and let out a cry. 'OH NO!' The little pot was still bubbling over with porridge. The porridge was pouring over the edge of the pot, it was running all over the table, down the legs, and had filled all the floor of the little house up to the window.

Her chair was floating on a sea of porridge. She held on to the edge of the table and called out to Ragamuffin. You see, she had forgotten the words that would stop the little pot.

She did her best. She called out, 'Do stop all this,' and 'No more porridge,' and, 'That's enough,' but it was no good. More and more porridge kept bubbling out of the pot. It poured through the windows and under the door, it swept through the streets of the little village like a great wave. It swept up under the doors and through the windows of the other villagers, and gradually all the village houses filled up with porridge. One by one the people struggled out through their front doors or windows. Their clothes were covered in the sticky porridge, but goodness it did taste delicious.

At that moment Ragamuffin came home. She shook her head as she stepped through the river of porridge; she had to try hard to keep from bursting out laughing. Just then her greedy mother came floating out of the window on her chair. 'Oh, help, Ragamuffin,' she called out. Then Ragamuffin and all the villagers laughed, and Ragamuffin said, 'Enough, little pot,' and the flow of porridge stopped, and her mother's chair came to a slow and sticky halt.

It took the village the rest of the winter to eat their way through all the lovely porridge. But at least nobody went hungry that year.

Little Bo-Peep

Little Bo-Peep has lost her sheep,
And doesn't know where to find them;
Leave them alone, and they'll come home,
Bringing their tails behind them.

Little Bo-Peep fell fast asleep,
And dreamt she heard them bleating;
For when she awoke, she found it a joke,
For they were still a-fleeting.

Then up she took her little crook,
Determined for to find them;
She found them indeed, but it made her
    heart bleed,
For they'd left their tails behind them.

It happened one day, as Bo-Peep did stray
Into a meadow hard by,
There she espied their tails side by side,
All hung on a tree to dry.

She heaved a sigh, and wiped her eye,
And over the hillocks went rambling,
And tried what she could, as a shepherdess
    should,
To tack each again to its lambkin.

Cuckoo, Cuckoo

Cuckoo, cuckoo,
What do you do?
In April
I open my bill;
In May
I sing night and day;
In June
I change my tune;
In July
Away I fly;
In August
Away I must.

There Was an Old Crow

There was an old crow
   Sat upon a clod;
That's the end of my song.
   —That's odd.

How Doth the Little Crocodile

How doth the little crocodile
Improve his shining tail,
And pour the waters of the Nile
On every golden scale!

How cheerfully he seems to grin,
How neatly spreads his claws,
And welcomes little fishes in,
With gently smiling jaws!

Lewis Carroll

If You Should Meet a Crocodile

If you should meet a crocodile,
Don't take a stick and poke him;
Ignore the welcome in his smile,
Be careful not to stroke him.
For as he sleeps upon the Nile,
He thinner gets and thinner;
But whene'er you meet a crocodile
He's ready for his dinner.

Jumping Joan

Here am I,
Little jumping Joan,
When nobody's with me,
I'm all alone.

Jack

Jack be nimble,
Jack be quick,
Jack jump over
The candlestick.

Peter Piper

Peter Piper picked a peck
of pickled pepper corns.
Where are those pickled pepper corns
that Peter Piper picked?

She Sells Sea-Shells on the Sea Shore

She sells sea-shells on the sea shore;
The shells she sells are sea-shells I'm sure.
So if she sells sea-shells on the sea shore,
I'm sure the shells are sea-shore shells.

Round and Round the Rugged Rock

Round and round the rugged rock
The ragged rascal ran.
How many R's are there in that?
Now tell me if you can.

Jack and the Beanstalk

Once upon a time, when there was still magic, there lived a boy called Jack. He lived with his mother in a little house on their farm. They were very poor, and the only possession they had left was Daisy the cow. Daisy was a very nice, but very old, cow and was the only real friend that Jack had. But one day Jack's mother said that it was no good, there was nothing left to eat, he must take Daisy to market and sell her or else they would starve.

The next morning Jack set off with Daisy, to walk to market. His mother waved them goodbye, and said, 'You make sure you get a good price, you know what a fool you are.'

Jack was sad to be selling Daisy, so he walked very slowly, hoping to be too late for the market. After a while they met an old man walking in the opposite direction. He was a very odd man; he was bent almost double and wore strange clothes, all coloured in green.

'Good morning, boy,' said the old man. 'What a fine cow. Where are you taking her?'

'I must take her to market and sell her, for we are very poor,' said Jack with a sigh.

'I never saw such a splendid animal,' said the old man. 'I should like to buy her myself.' And with that he reached into his green purse, and pulled out five beans.

Now, Jack had hoped for some gold coins. 'Those are beans,' he said. 'I couldn't sell Daisy for beans.'

'Ah,' said the old man, 'but these are magic beans. Plant these in your garden by moonlight and you will see.'

Jack was a trusting boy and he sold Daisy to the strange old man for the five magic beans.

His mother called him a fool. It was worse than she had feared, she said, now they would really starve. But Jack believed the old man, and that night, under the full moon, he planted the five beans.

His mother woke him early with a clout on the head. 'Now look what you've done!' she cried.

Jack hopped out of bed, and into the garden. Those beans really had been magic. Where he had planted them there now stood an enormous beanstalk with huge leaves. It stretched up into the sky and beyond the clouds. Jack saw at once a chance for adventure and perhaps even a fortune. Straightaway he began to climb.

Up and up he went, higher and higher, until he found himself above the clouds and in a different world.

Ahead of him stretched a long twisty road turning among the clouds and at the end of the road stood a huge castle. Jack walked up to the castle and climbed the steep steps to the door.

'Whoever lives here must be a giant,' said Jack to himself. He slipped into the castle through a crack in the door and found himself in a vast room with a fire blazing and a big table with legs made of tree trunks.

By the table was a wooden cage and in the cage Jack could see a fat white goose tied by a rope. 'Honk! Help me escape from here,' said the goose, 'and you will never be poor again, for I am a magic goose.'

Now Jack had good reason to believe in magic; the old man had been right about the beans after all. 'All right,' said Jack. 'I'll have you out of there in no time.'

But as he started to pull on the bars there came a sound like thunder,

BOOM . . .

BOOM . . .

BOOM,

and with it a voice low and loud . . .

Fee Fi Fo Fum

I smell the blood of a British man

Be he alive or be he dead

I'll grind his bones to make my bread.

'Quick,' said the goose, 'here comes the giant. Now hide where you can.' So Jack climbed up to the table top and hid behind a huge egg-cup. The door crashed open and in walked a terrible giant. He sat at the table, banged down his great fist, and laughed, 'Ho, ho, ho . . . where is my lovely goosey-goosey?'

The giant leaned down and picked up the cage and the goose. He pulled open the door, sat the poor goose in the middle of the table, and boomed out, 'Lay, goose, lay.' And the goose let out a sad 'honk', and laid an egg.

The giant picked up the egg and laughed again, 'Ho, ho, ho', and then carefully put the egg in the egg-cup. It was an egg of solid gold. Jack stared—it really was a magic goose. 'Lay, goose, lay,' said the giant again, and again the goose laid a golden egg, and so on until it had laid six eggs in all. Jack watched as the giant gradually fell asleep with a big smile on his face.

Jack crept out from behind the egg-cup and quickly untied the rope from the goose's neck. 'Climb on my back,' said the goose. And with Jack on her back she flew up and out of the castle window.

The flap of her wings woke the giant with a start, and as they flew down the road towards the beanstalk, the giant blundered after them, calling out, 'Goosey-goosey, come back.'

Jack hurled himself down the beanstalk, while the goose flew down beside him. But the giant started to climb down the beanstalk as well and his weight caused it to sway this way and that. Jack saw his mother at the bottom of the beanstalk and he called out to her to fetch the axe. As soon as Jack reached the ground he took the axe and chopped, until the beanstalk and the giant crashed to the ground. The giant, being so heavy, made such a hole that he fell right through the earth and was never seen again.

When Jack's mother saw the huge goose she was cross again. 'Whatever is that gert ugly bird?' she said. 'We can hardly feed ourselves let alone a gert thing like that.'

'It's a magic goose,' said Jack. 'Just you watch this. "Lay, goose, lay," ' he said to the goose, and patted it kindly on the head. The goose let out a happy 'honk' and laid a single golden egg, as it did once a year every year from then on. And so Jack, and his mother, and the goose, lived happily in comfort for the rest of their days.

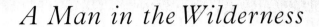

A Man in the Wilderness

A man in the wilderness asked me,
How many strawberries grow in the sea?
I answered him, as I thought good,
As many red herrings as swim in the wood.

If All the World Was Paper

If all the world was paper,
    And all the sea was ink,
If all the trees were bread and cheese,
    What should we have to drink?

Roses are Red

Roses are red,
  Violets are blue,
Sugar is sweet
  And so are you.

Lilies are White

Lilies are white,
  Rosemary's green,
When I am king,
  You shall be queen.

A Cat Came Fiddling

A cat came fiddling out of a barn,
With a pair of bagpipes under her arm,
She could sing nothing but 'Fiddle-de-dee.
The mouse has married the bumble bee.'
Pipe, cat—dance, mouse—
We'll have a wedding at our good house.

Sing, Sing

Sing, sing,
    What shall I sing?
The cat's run away
    With the pudding string!
Do, do,
    What shall I do?
The cat's run away
    With the pudding too!

The Common Cormorant

The common cormorant or shag
Lays eggs inside a paper bag
The reason you will see no doubt
It is to keep the lightning out.
But what these unobservant birds
Have never noticed is that herds
Of wandering bears may come with buns
And steal the bags to hold the crumbs.

Humpty Dumpty

Humpty Dumpty sat on a wall,
Humpty Dumpty had a great fall;
Humpty Dumpty lies in the beck
With a white counterpane round
　his neck.
All the King's horses and all the
　King's men
Can't put Humpty together again.

Higglety Pigglety

Higglety pigglety pop
The dog has eaten the mop
The pig's in a hurry
The cat's in a flurry
Higglety pigglety pop

Twinkle, Twinkle, Little Bat

Twinkle, twinkle, little bat!
How I wonder what you're at?
Up above the world you fly,
Like a tea-tray in the sky.

Lewis Carroll

The Story of the Elves and the Shoemaker

O nce upon a time, when the world was young and snow fell every winter, there lived a shoemaker and his wife. He was a fine craftsman, but recently trade had not been good, and they were very poor—so much so that the shoemaker had only one piece of leather left in his workshop, enough to make just one pair of shoes. So, that evening, he sat in his cold workshop and cut out the pieces of leather into all the shapes needed to make a pair of shoes.

Then his wife called him in for their supper, and so he wearily left all the cut-out pieces on his bench ready to make up in the morning.

He and his wife made a poor supper together of watery cabbage soup and scraps, and then, with their last stub of candle, lit their way to bed.

When the shoemaker opened his workshop door in the morning he had the shock of his life. There on the bench, instead of the cut-out patterns of leather, stood as fine a pair of shoes as he had ever seen. At first he suspected a trick. He looked under the bench for the bits of leather, but there was nothing, everything was just as tidy and spare as always. He called to his wife to come, and he fetched his glass lens that he sometimes used for especially close work. Together they looked at the shoes. It was his leather all right.

'Made by a master hand, much finer than my own,' he said. 'Even my old teacher couldn't make stitches so small and neat. But where are they from?'

'No matter,' said his wife. ''Tis divine providence. These shoes will make our fortune, you'll see.' So saying, she put the shoes in the middle of the shop window.

It was not long before the shoes were noticed. A customer came in and tried them on. Walking up and down the shop, he said they were the most comfortable and handsome shoes he had ever worn, and he happily paid twice the normal price for them. Now there was enough money to buy leather to make two pairs of shoes, and even some left over for a good supper.

That evening, the shoemaker cut out the leather and left the pieces ready for making up in the morning; and that night the soup was thicker and tastier, and the shoemaker and his wife went to bed well satisfied. And sure enough, in the morning, when the shoemaker opened his workshop, there were two pairs of perfectly made shoes, all complete with their tiny stitching, and the leather soft and glossy with polish.

The shoes were soon sold, and the shoemaker was able to buy enough leather to make four pairs of shoes. Again the shoemaker carefully cut out the patterns, and again in the morning there stood four more pairs of exquisite shoes, and so it went on.

The shoemaker was able to buy more and more leather in all the colours of the rainbow. He cut out a great variety of shoes, and pumps, and slippers, and boots. Every morning he would come in to find them all perfectly finished as before.

He was soon thought to be the best shoemaker in the land, and one morning the king himself arrived with his page and chancellor and bought an especially fine pair of high boots in green leather.

One night the shoemaker and his wife could contain their curiosity no longer. They decided to hide themselves in the workshop and keep watch, just to see what sort of providence was at work. They left a tall candle lit near a pile of recently cut patterns on the workbench, and then settled in their hiding place to wait.

When the clock chimed midnight a pair of strange little figures climbed up on to the workbench. They were tiny, not much bigger than a shoe themselves, and they wore very odd clothes: acorn halves for hats, leaves and grasses and scraps for clothes. 'Elves,' whispered the shoemaker. But his wife shushed him and they settled to watch the elves at work.

The elves worked hard and fast, they stitched with tiny needles, and hammered with tiny hammers, and buffed and polished with little cloths. They worked on as the clock chimed the night hours. They didn't stop until the candle was almost burnt down and daylight showed through the frosty window. Then the two elves scuttled back under the door, leaving a line of beautiful shoes on the bench.

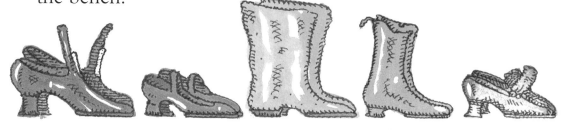

The shoemaker and his wife crept out of their hiding place. 'Did you ever see anything like it?' said the shoemaker. 'Those elves have helped us to make our fortune. And did you see what they were wearing? Just little scraps, and acorns, and bits and bobs. They must be frozen in this weather.' And the shoemaker and his wife shook their heads.

'I have an idea,' said the shoemaker's wife. 'We shall make some fine clothes for them, as a way of saying thank you.'

So, during the day, (which was Christmas Eve), the shoemaker and his wife cut and sewed with their nimble fingers. They made some little shirts, and waistcoats, and jackets, and breeches, and even stockings and mittens. They used pieces of brocade, and velvet, and

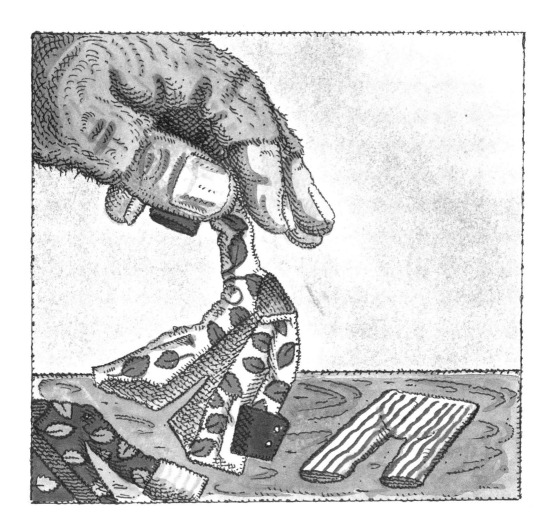

silk, and cambric, and fine wool. That night they laid out all the little clothes on the workbench, and settled themselves in their hiding place to wait.

Sure enough, as the clock chimed midnight the two elves appeared. They climbed up to the workbench, where they found all the fine new clothes, beautifully cut and sewn. The elves happily put on their new clothes, laughing and chattering to themselves.

'Happy Christmas, little men,' whispered the shoemaker and his wife.

Then the elves danced round the candlestick, and as they danced they sang,

Now we're dressed so fine and neat
We'll no more work for other's feet.

And then they danced off the bench, under the door, and were never seen again.

The shoemaker and his wife hung a smart new sign on the front of their shop; it was cut out in the shape of an elegant shoe, and had 'By Royal Appointment' painted on it in crisp gold letters. The shoemaker and his wife lived happily and prospered until the end of their days, which was a very long time indeed.

Snow

A milk-white bird
Floats down through the air.
And never a tree
But he lights there.

An Egg

In marble walls as white as milk,
Lined with a skin as soft as silk,
Within a fountain crystal-clear,
A golden apple doth appear.
No doors there are to this stronghold,
Yet thieves break in and steal the gold.

Christmas

Christmas is coming
The goose is getting fat,
Please to put a penny
In the old man's hat.
If you haven't got a penny
A ha'penny will do,
If you haven't got a ha'penny,
God bless you.

We Wish You a Merry Christmas

We wish you a merry Christmas,
We wish you a merry Christmas,
We wish you a merry Christmas,
And a happy New Year.
Good tidings we bring
To you and your kin.
We wish you a merry Christmas
And a happy New Year.

Little Jack Horner

Little Jack Horner
Sat in a corner,
Eating a Christmas pie;
He put in his thumb,
And pulled out a plum,
And said, 'What a good boy am I!'

Jingle Bells

Dashing thro' the snow
In a one-horse open sleigh;
O'er the fields we go,
Laughing all the way.
Bells on Bobtail ring,
Making spirits bright;
What fun it is to ride and sing
A sleighing song tonight!

Jingle bells, jingle bells,
Jingle all the way.
O! What fun it is to ride
In a one-horse open sleigh.

Jingle bells, jingle bells,
Jingle all the way.
O! What fun it is to ride
In a one-horse open sleigh.

I Sing of a Maiden

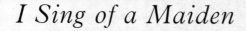

I sing of a maiden
That is makeless;
King of all kings
To her son she chose.

He came all so still
There his mother was,
As dew in April
That falleth on the grass.

He came all so still
To his mother's bower,
As dew in April
That falleth on the flower.

He came all so still
There his mother lay,
As dew in April
That falleth on the spray.

Mother and maiden
Was never none but she;
Well may such a lady
God's mother be.

I Saw Three Ships Come Sailing By

I saw three ships come sailing by,
Come sailing by, come sailing by,
I saw three ships come sailing by,
On Christmas Day in the morning.

And what do you think was in them then,
Was in them then, was in them then,
And what do you think was in them then,
On Christmas Day in the morning?

Three pretty girls were in them then,
Were in them then, were in them then,
Three pretty girls were in them then,
On Christmas Day in the morning.

One could whistle, and one could sing,
And one could play on the violin;
Such joy there was at my wedding,
On Christmas Day in the morning.

The Sound of the Wind

The wind has such a rainy sound
Moaning through the town,
The sea has such a windy sound,
Will the ships go down?

The apples in the orchard
Tumble from their tree.
Oh will the ships go down, go down,
In the windy sea?

Christina Rossetti

Blow, Wind, Blow

Blow, wind, blow!
And go, mill, go!
That the miller may grind his corn;
That the baker may take it,
And into bread make it,
And bring us a loaf in the morn.

The Princess and
the Pea

Once upon a time, in a faraway kingdom, there lived a prince. He was an only child, and spoilt a little by his parents. For his twentieth birthday he was given a fine white stallion, called Blaze. One day his father sent for the prince. 'My boy,' he said, 'it is time you set out and found yourself a real princess to marry.' So the prince travelled the length and breadth of the world on Blaze. They rode through summer sun and winter snow. They rode under all the phases of the moon, through deserts and over mountains.

The prince met many girls who said that they were princesses. Girls who curtsied very nicely. Girls with eyes hidden behind painted fans. Girls who danced elegantly in bright, silk dresses. But the prince was never sure if any of them was a real princess. The king and queen had insisted, 'She must be a real princess.' But after all his travels, the prince had never been sure whether any of the girls he had met had been a real princess.

And so, one night, under a new moon, the prince rode back into the palace yard, with his head bowed and a heavy heart. His mother welcomed him back with his favourite meal. 'Come on,' she said, 'sausages, onion gravy, and mashed potatoes. I cooked them myself, this ought to cheer you up.'

But although the prince made a hearty supper, he was still sad. 'I've looked over the whole world, from one end to the other. I'll never find a real princess,' and he sighed.

'Don't worry,' said the queen, 'there are ways of telling a real princess. When the right girl comes, I will find out for you, never fear.'

Summer turned to autumn, and great storms shook the kingdom. Hailstones the size of goose eggs crashed around the palace turrets. A great wind tore up the ancient oak that the prince had played in since his childhood. Then winter came, howling in on a blizzard, and the palace was surrounded with deep drifts of snow; even Blaze was kept in the stable under fleecy blankets.

Then one night, the coldest of the year so far, when even the powdered snow had frozen into hard ice, there was a knocking at the palace door. The king was roused from his warm fireside. 'Who on earth can that be out in this awful weather, and at this late hour?' He set off, wrapped in his warmest cloak, and opened the heavy door.

A girl stood knee deep in a drift of snow. Her fine cape, reduced to rags, was wrapped around her shoulders, and she was huddled and shivering. Her hair was wet around her face, and there were little icicles on her sooty eyelashes. She fell into the king's arms, and he carried her into the warm parlour.

After a few minutes the girl was warmed through. She sat by the fire, drinking a cup of hot chocolate. Some colour had come back into her cheeks, and as she brushed the strands of damp hair away from her face, the prince could see that she might just be beautiful.

The queen stole a glance at her son, and noticed that he was a little smitten with the mysterious girl. 'Tell us about yourself, my dear,' said the queen.

'I am Princess Phoebe,' said the girl. 'I have been travelling the world, seeking a suitable prince to marry.' She shook her head sadly. 'I had searched for nearly a year with no luck, for you see he must be a real prince. I was just on my way home when the blizzard struck. I stabled my poor horse, and then followed the lights here.'

The prince was about to speak out when the queen gestured to him to be quiet. Then she said brightly, 'Well, my dear, you must be exhausted. You must have a hot bath, then we will put you to bed, and in the morning all shall be well.'

While Phoebe was in her bath, the queen took the prince and two servants to the guest bedchamber. She ordered the servants to strip all the bedding from the bed, and start over again. When the mattress was removed the queen took a little silver box from her purse, opened the box, and inside was a single green pea.

The queen took the pea and placed it in the middle of the bed base. Then she ordered the servants to bring as many mattresses and feather quilts as could be found. She had all the mattresses piled one on top of the other, along with all the quilts and covers. When they had finished there must have been fifty or more, reaching almost to the ceiling, and it was a very tall room.

'Now we shall see if she is a real princess,' said the queen. 'Trust me.'

Princess Phoebe spent an uncomfortable night. Despite the duvets, feather mattresses, and cosy warmth, things weren't right. No matter how she lay in the bed, no matter how she twisted and turned, this way and that, it was no good, she couldn't settle, and through all that night she didn't sleep a wink.

In the morning, all looked beautiful in the bright sunshine. This would be a fine place to live, Phoebe thought, looking across the snow-covered kingdom from the high window. She went down to the parlour for breakfast.

'Good morning, my dear,' said the queen. 'I hope you slept well.'

Phoebe looked tired, and her eyes had dark circles round them. 'I have never spent a more uncomfortable night,' she said. 'I couldn't sleep at all. No matter how I lay in the bed it felt as if something was digging into me.

I must be covered in bruises.'

It was then that the prince understood what his mother had been doing. If this girl had felt such a tiny thing as a pea through all those layers of quilts and feathers, then she must be a real princess.

'Look around you, my dear,' said the queen. 'You will see that this is no ordinary house, it is a palace.'

Phoebe looked at all the silverware on the breakfast table; the fine damasks and silks at the tall windows. At that moment the king entered, dressed in his state robes and accompanied by his lord chamberlain, who carried a crown on a velvet cushion.

'If this is a palace,' said Phoebe, 'then you must be the queen, and there, if I am not mistaken, is the king.' At that she curtsied, and then bounced up with a smile on her face. 'Which means that your son is a real prince.'

Later that day the princess's horse was brought from the stables, a fine black mare with a long silky tail. Together the prince and princess set off to ride in the bright winter sunshine. There was even a promise of spring in the air. 'Mark my words,' said the queen, 'we'd best set the lord chamberlain to preparing the cathedral for a royal wedding.'

And so they did, and later that year the real prince and the real princess were married, and went to live in their own palace by a lake with a good stable for both their fine horses. Soon they had to add a nursery, and so they all lived happily to the end of their days, which was as long a time as it could be.

Rock-a-Bye, Baby

Rock-a-bye, baby,
  Thy cradle is green,
Father's a nobleman,
  Mother's a queen;
And Betty's a lady,
  And wears a gold ring;
And Johnny's a drummer,
  And drums for the king.

Golden Slumbers

Golden slumbers
Kiss your eyes,
Smiles await you
When you rise,
Sleep little baby,
Don't you cry,
And I will sing a lullaby.

Infant Joy

'I have no name;
'I am but two days old.'
What shall I call thee?
'I happy am;
'Joy is my name.'
Sweet joy befall thee!

Pretty joy!
Sweet joy but two days old,
Sweet joy I call thee.
Thou dost smile,
I sing the while.
Sweet joy befall thee!

William Blake

African Lullaby

Sleep, sleep, my little one! The night is all wind and rain;
The meal has been wet by the raindrops and bent is the sugar cane;
O Giver who gives to the people, in safety my little son keep!
My little son with the head-dress, sleep, sleep, sleep!

What Do the Stars Do?

What do the stars do
Up in the sky,
Higher than the wind can blow
Or the clouds can fly?

Each star in its own glory
Circles, circles still,
As it was lit to shine and set,
And do its Maker's will.

Twinkle, Twinkle, Little Star

Twinkle, twinkle, little star,
How I wonder what you are!
Up above the world so high,
Like a diamond in the sky.

Jane and Ann Taylor

My Bed is a Boat

My bed is like a little boat;
Nurse helps me in when I embark;
She girds me in my sailor's coat
And starts me in the dark.

At night, I go on board and say
Goodnight to all my friends on shore;
I shut my eyes and sail away
And see and hear no more.

And sometimes things to bed I take,
As prudent sailors have to do:
Perhaps a slice of wedding-cake,
Perhaps a toy or two.

All night across the dark we steer:
But when the day returns at last,
Safe in my room, beside the pier,
I find my vessel fast.

Robert Louis Stevenson

Rock-a-Bye Baby

Rock-a-bye baby on the tree top,
When the wind blows the cradle will rock;
When the bough breaks the cradle will fall,
Down will come baby, cradle and all.

O Lady Moon

O Lady Moon, your horns point towards the east:
Shine, be increased;
O Lady Moon, your horns point towards the west:
Wane, be at rest.

Christina Rossetti

Night

The sun descending in the west,
The evening star does shine;
The birds are silent in their nest,
And I must seek for mine.
The moon, like a flower,
In heaven's high bower,
With silent delight
Sits and smiles on the night.

Farewell, green fields and happy groves
Where flocks have took delight;
Where lambs have nibbled, silent moves
The feet of angels bright.
Unseen they pour blessing,
And joy without ceasing,
On each bud and blossom,
And each sleeping bosom.

William Blake

Star Wish

Star light, star bright,
First star I see tonight,
I wish I may, I wish I might,
Have the wish I wish tonight.